## A NOTE TO THE READER

HOMOGRAPHS are words that are spelled the same but pronounced differently and have different meanings, such as TEAR (to cry) and TEAR (to rip).

HOMONYMS are words that sound the same and are spelled the same but have different meanings, such as BOWL (a round dish) and BOWL (the sport).

HOMOPHONES are words that sound the same but are spelled differently and have different meanings, such as TALE (a story) and TAIL (a part of an animal).

For my favorite band, Brother Billy & The Uncles: Billy (vocals), Paul (guitar), Harry (drums), Phil (piano), Alan (bass), Uncle (banjo), and Jim (violin) —Love, G

This book was originally published under the title *Zoola Palooza*.

Henry Holt and Company, *Publishers since 1866*
Henry Holt® is a registered trademark of Macmillan Publishing Group, LLC
175 Fifth Avenue, New York, NY 10010
mackids.com

Library of Congress Cataloging-in-Publication Data

Names: Barretta, Gene, author, illustrator.
Title: The bass plays the bass and other homographs / Gene Barretta.
Other titles: Zoola palooza
Description: New York : Henry Holt and Company, [2018] | "Christy Ottaviano Books." | "Originally published in 2011 by Henry Holt under the title Zoola Palooza." | Summary: Playing a variety of musical instruments, animals on a concert tour introduce words that are spelled the same but sound different and have different meanings, such as tear (to cry) and tear (to rip).
Identifiers: LCCN 2018009010 | ISBN 9781250175076 (hardcover)
Subjects: | CYAC: English language—Homonyms—Fiction. | Animals—Fiction. | Concerts—Fiction. | Musicians—Fiction.
Classification: LCC PZ7.B275366 Bas 2018 | DDC [E]—dc23
LC record available at https://lccn.loc.gov/2018009010

Our books may be purchased in bulk for promotional, educational, or business use. Please contact your local bookseller or the Macmillan Corporate and Premium Sales Department (800) 221-7945 ext. 5442 or by e-mail at MacmillanSpecialMarkets@macmillan.com.

Watercolor on Arches cold-press paper was used to create the illustrations for this book.
Printed in China by RR Donnelley Asia Printing Solutions Ltd., Dongguan City, Guangdong Province

1 3 5 7 9 10 8 6 4 2

# THE BASS PLAYS THE BASS AND OTHER HOMOGRAPHS

## GENE BARRETTA

Christy Ottaviano Books
Henry Holt and Company
NEW YORK

ENTRANCE
and
CRICKETS
TICKETS

Have you **READ** about the greatest
music festival in the animal kingdom?
We just saw it! **READ** my shirt—
"Zoola Palooza. No cages. Just stages."

Billy the striped **BASS** opened the show
wearing a big striped **BOW** tie.
He took a gracious **BOW** from the top
of his **BASS** fiddle.

Carter Piller was on stage NUMBER two.

He played a 30-MINUTE solo with a guitar

that was so loud and yet so MINUTE.

His fingers were numb—

but our ears were NUMBER.

The drummer for The Catnip Clan was exhausted.

Usually that cat lives to REBEL.

But today he was just

a REBEL without his claws.

Carmen Chameleon's **ENTRANCE** will **ENTRANCE** you. She's the only singer we know who can **PRODUCE** a fresh bowl of **PRODUCE** and blend into it.

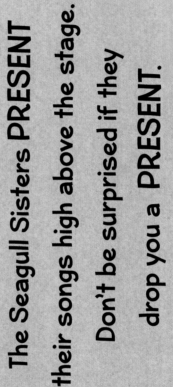
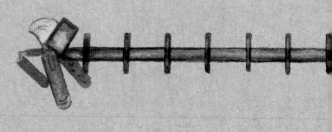

**The Seagull Sisters PRESENT**

their songs high above the stage.

Don't be surprised if they

drop you a PRESENT.

There will be no official
**RECORD** of the show.
The sound engineers forgot
to press the **RECORD** button.

The scariest moment was when
Sally Mander dressed up like a DOVE
and DOVE into the audience.
Fortunately, she WOUND up landing
on the back of a jellyfish, WOUND-free.

They had to CONSOLE the worried stage crew after the power CONSOLE blew up. But the light show was amazing!

Florence Welk had a fresh coat of POLISH
on her POLKA-dot accordion.

As soon as she played it, everyone danced
the POLKA and waved the POLISH flag.

The Crying Crocodiles gave
**TEAR**-stained towels to everyone.
We're going to **TEAR** ours into pieces
and make more Croco-Dolls.

DOES The Dear Deer Band have
the PERFECT fan club?
Yes! They call themselves The Fa-So-La-Te-DOES
and spend hours trying to PERFECT their antlers.

The crowd was pretty rowdy at The Rabbits show.

Fluff Daddy stopped and shouted,

"EXCUSE me. There's no EXCUSE for that!

Do I have to SEPARATE you guys

and give you each a SEPARATE time-out?"

Hedda Hip-Hopper was a prime
SUSPECT in today's big scandal.
We SUSPECT someone else
was doing her singing.

Seals & Crawfish always CLOSE the concert
the same way. They WIND up their Victrola and
blow crawfish out of their WIND instruments.
If you're hungry, sit up CLOSE.

So there's no USE hanging around. We'll USE
these tickets and follow the show from town to town.
We'll LIVE in our car and get Daddy to drive.
Because nothing beats seeing . . .